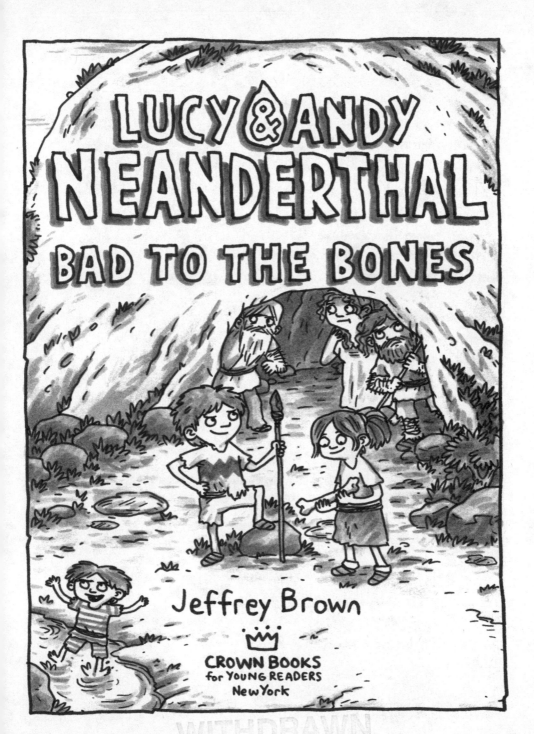

LUCY & ANDY NEANDERTHAL
BAD TO THE BONES

Jeffrey Brown

CROWN BOOKS
for YOUNG READERS
New York

Did you figure out the deal with these words yet, Eric?

I have some theories, Pam, but I need to read more books to figure it out!

Thank you to my family, friends, publishers, and readers for all of their support. Thanks also to Marc, Phoebe, and everyone at RH for making this book happen. And special thanks to Kevin Lee for giving me the nudge that led to the idea for this book.

For his expert assistance, grateful acknowledgment to Jonathan S. Mitchell, PhD, Evolutionary Biology, and member of the Geological Society of America, Society of Vertebrate Paleontology, and Society for the Study of Evolution.

All rights reserved. Published in the United States by Crown Books for Young Readers, an imprint of Random House Children's Books, a division of Penguin Random House LLC, New York.

Crown and the colophon are registered trademarks of Penguin Random House LLC.

Visit us on the Web! rhcbooks.com

Educators and librarians, for a variety of teaching tools, visit us at RHTeachersLibrarians.com

Library of Congress Cataloging-in-Publication Data is available upon request.
ISBN 978-0-385-38841-2 (trade) — ISBN 978-0-385-38843-6 (lib. bdg.) — ISBN 978-0-385-38842-9 (ebook)

Printed in the United States of America
10 9 8 7 6 5 4 3 2 1
First Edition

3

Now it's spring, the cave bear is gone, and Lucy is looking forward to new adventures with her friends...

Do you want to look for rocks or sticks?

...while Andy hopes to take the next step in becoming a leader like his dad.

Follow me to victory!

Victory over what?

Uh, over defeat?

It's going to be a good year — if they can stay out of each other's way!

BONK!

If you want to go with Lucy, you'll need to finish your chores, too, Andy.

I did, Dad!

Fixed my clothes, organized my tools.

It depends on how you define "fixed" and "organized."

I just need to do my most important job of all....

Stop smelling up our cave?

No, Margaret! I have to be Lucy's armed guard on the way to Sasha's cave.

Like I said, you leave and our cave stops smelling.

You can go with them, Margaret. Oh, and taking Danny with you — good idea, Lucy.

What?

Oh, Danny's been attached to my leg so long, I forgot he was there.

Good. You can carry him, then.

10

In modern humans, hay fever is a seasonal allergy that causes runny noses and watery eyes.

Research shows that Neanderthals had allergies very much like ours.

There are no studies on how much Neanderthals wiped their noses on their sleeves!

AH-CHOO!

DODGE!

Wahhhhh!

Andy! You woke up Sasha's sister!

No, Tara was already up. Andy just surprised her.

She's surprised someone can have a snottier nose than she does.

Sniff.

Maybe I AM allergic to Rithard... Ah-AH—

Heh, heh!

I would high-five you, but I'm afraid your hand is slimy.

17

THE SUPER ADVENTURE EXPLORERS DISCOVERY CLUB!!

Ha,ha,ha! The Super Goofballs Dork Club is more like it!

Can I join?

Nope.

Not with that attitude, Richard. If I know adventure, and I do, you—

You can't join either, Andy.

Oh, I see. It's a girls-only club.

No, everyone else can join.

Mostly it's Andy and Richard who can't join.

It's an adventure club, not a drama club.

The only drama is from Andy! You're the one who starts it!

No, I mind my own business and—

What?

No drama, huh?

Maybe we'll start our OWN club.

ClubS. I'm not going to be in a club with you.

That's fine, but can you take all the clubs outside? I want quiet while Danny is napping.

Hey, it stopped raining!

25

Good job, Richard. Now we're getting special punishment.

No, this is part of your training. You need to learn how to work together.

We're getting special training? What spears do we use?

You don't need spears.

We're learning how to hunt with our bare hands? This is the kind of intense training I'm ready for!

In the first exercise, you two will play the role of the deer.

You're kidding.

Does it look like I'm kidding?

You always have the same sulky expression, so we can't tell.

Let me see your deer impressions.

NOW.

uh, we're frolicking in the grass?

Prance, prance.

27

Rustle
Rustle

AAAAHHHHH!

EEEEEKK!!

Wait up! We're supposed to work together!

We're the deer, Andy! Deer don't work together!

This is survival of the fittest!

AUGGHH!

AAAHHHH!

Humans have bodies suited for running. Scientists think early humans may have hunted in open spaces where it's easier to track animals, and chased their prey until it was tired.

Neanderthals may have specialized in ambushing animals and killing them at close quarters.

Prey most likely didn't drop dead from surprise, and so still needed to be killed.

38

39

It seems like you guys are making this up as you go.

Definitely not! But I can see how you'd think that, since our Motto is "If you don't have it, Make it!"

Everyone, grab your walking sticks and let's head out!

That's not a stick, Richard.

Sure it is. It just has a pointy end.

I have two sticks with pointy ends.

Why do you need two?

I don't, but it looks cool.

Where are we going?

Exploring, dummy.

I know. I mean, WHERE?

Let's see what we can find down by the river.

Hurry, before Margaret tries to make us take Danny.

45

It's not really exploring if we know where we're going. Why don't we wander off that way?

You mean into that patch of poison ivy?

Not there SPECIFICALLY. Just wherever. Like, over in that direction.

Ohhhh! Into the grove of poison oak?

No! Just somewhere that isn't poisonous and we haven't been to!

Whenever it rains a lot, we find interesting stuff by the river!

Really? Maybe WE should go to the river!

Ha, ha! Just kidding.

Unless there's some interesting food there.

46

47

Dinosaurs last roamed the earth about 65 million years ago — long before humans and Neanderthals appeared!

In 1841, the scientist Richard Owen came up with the name Dinosauria for their fossils, which means "terrible lizards."

I'm not so terrible!

People were aware of dinosaur fossils hundreds of years ago but had no idea what they really were. They thought the bones might be from mythical creatures — dinosaurs may have been the origin of stories about dragons!

Maybe Neanderthals found dinosaur skulls! Unfortunately, they didn't make any cave paintings of them.

Mammoths have trunks. It's probably some kind of cat, like Tiny. Like a... mega-Tiny!

It could be a new <u>kind</u> of mammoth!

Or a giant reptile with wings that breathes fire and collects precious treasure that it piles in the cave where it lives.

Tommy, your imagination is both inspiring and terrifying.

We should bring the bones back and ask Mr. Daryl.

Yeah. He'll know. He probably saw these things around when he was a kid.

55

The terrible horror is really small.

The water must have shrunk the monster before it came back to life.

Ribbit.

It's a frog! I'm going to call him Hoppy.

HE could be a SHE, you know.

I think Tiny would like to call it lunch. Hoppy wouldn't taste good, Tiny. I know from experience.

Ew.

You can play with your pet frog later, Tommy. Help us dig.

How are we going to lift that?! We can all lift together. This will look great in my cave spot!

There's not enough room in your cave, Andy. Plus, the club HQ is in our cave. True.

58

Claire, what did Phil mean by "not safe"? Is it the strangers? Or these monster bones?

No, they think the longer you're out exploring, the more likely you'll get into trouble. So we're walking you home.

Well, I can't walk.

Carry me.

How are we going to carry Richard AND all of these bones?

We can make a sled!

Lash the bigger bones together, and we can drag the skull and other bones home.

And drag Richard by his arms?

Let go!

Richard can ride on top of this one.

Why didn't you think of something like this, Phil?

It's definitely not because I didn't want you kids to bring home all this junk.

61

68

Watch my head.

Where have you been? We were just talking about the Explorers Club's first major discovery.

You began the meeting already?!

scratch
scratch
scratch

Everyone else got here early, so we went ahead and started.

You didn't miss much. Mostly it was Tommy talking about—

Let me guess: cave bears.

No! Regular bears. And how they sometimes live in caves.

scratch
scratch

Are we going to research the bones now?

No, we'll wait and ask Mr. Daryl about them. We're in the exploring business, not analyzing.

I think Danny is old and tall enough now!

They grow up so fast.

Yay! Club!

There are too many people in the clubhouse. Let's get out of here.

Scratch scratch

Club? Club!

Scratch scratch

I just realized Danny thinks the "club" is the kind of "club" you hit things with.

I was wondering why he was so interested.

Club!

That would be more fun. When are we going to do more training?

When you're done taking care of me.

Scratch scratch Scratch

I need a drink of water.

Okay, but stop with all the scratching!

73

Since the 1950s, kids have used the word "cooties" for imaginary illness. The term comes from a real pest that has been around since before Neanderthals—lice!

ACTUAL SIZE

Head lice live only on the human scalp, but another species — body lice — live on skin and clothing.

Fortunately, you can get snuggles from pets, but not lice!

Neanderthal beds were made of grass and other plants, then covered with animal fur.

Cozy sleeping space ←

Because there were no washing machines, Neanderthals burned their beds instead! The new layer of ash helped keep bugs away and was softer than the hard ground.

The fire's just about out. You can get to work making our beds.

I'll make my bed. Why should I make yours?

scratch scratch

Richard has to do my chores for a week, and you have to take care of Richard. So you have to do my chores.

Good thing our club is all about teamwork. You can help me do your chores!

KIDS! What's going on?! Where's all this smoke coming from?!

You can take all the credit for this part.

scratch scratch

You kids go with Lucy's parents. We'll stay here to clean up this mess.

Can we bring our bones with us? We want to see if Mr. Daryl knows anything about them.

Sure!

Club?

But you have to carry them.

Never mind.

It's not like the bones will walk off on their own.

Lucy, why is Richard riding on Andy's back?

Do you really want to know?

Probably not.

81

We don't hunt deer until the fall. The fawns need to grow up first.

Does Andy know that? He thinks he's going on a deer hunt.

He knows if he's been paying attention to the hunts his whole life.

So he has no idea.

Rabbit soup will be great, though. Last week's rabbit soup was DELICIOUS!

That wasn't rabbit soup.

Really? What meat was in it, then?

There wasn't any meat in it. Just vegetables.

Are you sure?

What soup were YOU eating, Sasha?!

C'mon, Phil, just tell me where they went to hunt.

If I told you, I'd have to kill you.

Ha! So you don't know either!

I'm just showing you how much I care.

This won't take long. Here's a carrot!

And...that's it.

This is going to take _forever_. Too bad all the vegetables don't just grow right here.

Sasha! That's a brilliant idea!

How is taking forever a brilliant idea?

No, if all the plants grew nearby, it would be way easier to collect them!

Cool! How do we do that?

I have no idea!

Yeah, what are you going to do, bring the plants here and stick them in the ground where you want them to grow?

Great idea, Richard!

All we've eaten lately are vegetables. While you guys get overexcited about eating more, I'm going to...have some alone time.

Andy seems crankier than normal.

Sometimes he gets like that when he eats a lot of vegetables.

By studying teeth, bones, and poop, scientists know Neanderthals ate their veggies!

Fortunately, fossilized poop doesn't stink!

People digest food differently from other animals. By analyzing the composition of fossil poop, scientists can identify who created it, and determine what they ate.

Feel better?

Now that Andy's mission is complete, it's time for Mission: Veggies!

Aren't those poses overly dramatic for picking vegetables?

Dramatic poses are always appropriate!

This club sure does a lot.

But why do we need to call it a club? We did stuff before and just called it... doing stuff.

Exactly. Now that we're a club, it feels like we do MORE. Even if we don't.

Richard, it seems like your leg is feeling better.

Yeah.

So I guess you don't need me to take care of you anymore.

I mean, it's not totally fine yet. I'm just tolerating the pain.

Wasn't it his other leg that got hurt?

Ouch! Ow!

Ooh.

Ow.

I think we've found potatoes growing around here somewhere.... Is that one?

They don't grow on trees, Tommy.

Oh.

91

It has this thing on its nose.

Yeah. That's a mammoth.

No!

We know what a mammoth is! It's not a mammoth!

All that matters is that it's really fierce and we need you kids out of the way!

scratch scratch

Fine.

scratch scratch

What?

Oh, you mean out of the way, like, right now.

Yeah, you're standing in the middle of the path.

See ya later, kids.

Watch out for —

OUCH! Not again!

— the tree.

96

Neanderthals may have
taken hot baths!

Shallow pits in Neanderthal
caves may have held water.
Some of these pits contain
rocks that had cracks
← from being heated.

Scientists don't know if Neanderthal kids
complained about bathtime, though.

What if
I clean you?

splash!
splash!

WAHHHHHHH!!!

Andy, what did
you do to your
brother?

Mama!

I'm just
helping
him get
clean!

It's okay, Danny.

Andy naughty.

I know.

I feel like Mr. Daryl's vegetable
soup is missing something.

Everyone thinks babies are so cute, but they just sit there and don't even do anything.

Pffffbbftt!

Babies _are_ boring. They can't even talk, but grown-ups stare at them in awe.

Get used to it.

My parents are oblivious to everything around them when they think Danny's being cute.

Yeah. I try to talk to my mom, but she has this blank stare and just says "mm-hm" no matter what I say!

Unless they think you did something bad, and then they're all over you! Like - watch this.

Hey, Danny! This is my stick. You can't have it.

I want stick.

Nope. It's mine.

That's fine. Richard and I can go get some REAL training from Phil.

Not so fast!

Yeah. Not so fast.

You two can gather firewood for Mr. Daryl.

Didn't see that coming.

We'll show them. Let's collect the most, best firewood they've ever seen!

Andy, why do you love firewood so much?

I don't. My family does. It's like they can't live without it.

I mean, we can't live without it, probably. But still.

Yeah. They're totally obsessed.

Like moms and babies.

Yeah.

My mom would be happy if I was always out gathering firewood so she could just sit in the cave playing with Tara.

Here's a good one.

Or she'll make you help out in Lucy and Sasha's garden.

Or make a baby garden so all the babies are in the same place!

Here's a better one.

Richard, that's great!

It's great that my mom cares about babies and not me?

No... a baby garden! The garden of vegetables makes it easier to gather plants to eat, right?

Ooh, this is the best one yet.

Why would we want to grow more babies?

Not babies. ANIMALS! What if we made a garden of animals? Then we wouldn't have to go all over hunting them!

Wow, Andy, maybe you're not as dumb as I thought!

Maybe?

108

111

If they did this, it makes sense that a group of rhinos is called a crash.

Andy and Richard are a crash when they're together.

Where are they, anyway?

Right here!

I admired Roger's ambition before, but I'm not so sure now.

It's Richard.

scratch scratch

Andy? Richard? What happened?

scratch scratch

Well, that's a funny story.

Actually, it's not. I'm sure no one wants to hear it....

In Spain, scientists found evidence that Neanderthals may have used fires in funeral rituals. The fires had been lit for a burial.

Antlers and horns were also deliberately placed in the fires.

But there's no indication that Neanderthals had funerals for pets. And they didn't have toilets for flushing pet goldfish!

129

Tortoise shells with marks indicating they were roasted have been found in caves dating back almost 400,000 years ago.

Neanderthals may have mostly eaten large prey, but turtles and tortoises provided additional sources of meat.

Hunting tortoises wasn't as dangerous as hunting rhinos, but it would still hurt to drop one on your foot!

133

But don't you want to teach us a lesson by making us take care of it?

Yes...but why don't you think of how you can make it up to everyone?

I hate when parents do that. Whatever we think of is probably worse than what they would come up with!

Maybe not.

How about we just go with you to help?

Ha, ha, ha, ha, ha, ha!

No.

Besides, I have a bad feeling that a storm is headed our way....

Dad, when you say "storm," do you really mean something bad?

Like, the strangers are up to no good and they're going to cause trouble, no matter what?

And whatever happens could cause devastating damage with terrible noise and power?

Your mom and Mrs. Sylvia are going this time.

Dad, I think I need to explain what a catch is to you.

No, I know. They're going to catch the rhino!

We're going to stay here with all of you. Tara's a bit of a daddy's girl.

Plus, we all know I'm a better tracker than your dad.

Good luck!

Sure you don't need me to come with you, Mom? I can tell you which way—

—it went? You mean this way?

I wouldn't have predicted that your mom was psychic! Or they followed the obvious trail of destruction.

Oh.

I just realized we're going to be stuck here with the toddlers.

143

145

146

Maybe someday soon we can get a tour of that cave, too.

It sounds really great!

Keep taking care of yourselves!

Those guys are up to no good.

Definitely.

Just because they're strangers doesn't mean they're bad people.

Yeah. You guys were okay!

Then why do they want to see the other cave?

They like cave tours!

And why were they out in the rain?

We were out in the rain, too.

And they gave each other that sneaky "we've got an idea" look.

You two make that look all the time.

Exactly!

But why would they say "take care" when they left?

Did you not see the devious smile when he said that?!

Okay, maybe that was a little weird. And how they said "see you soon" while pointing at us with their spears and laughing evilly.

But Alan seemed so nice. He couldn't even remember your name.

So? Mom and Dad mix up our names all the time.

Why are we standing here arguing?!

Is it raining again?

Yeah, but we need to tell someone about the strangers!

Great. It's raining outside, and now it's raining kids inside.

Margaret! Oh my gosh!

Lucy! Oh my gosh! What?!

This isn't a time for jokes. Something serious is going on!

Like what? The strangers are planning to raid our caves, take our stuff and leave us out to dry?

No! Er, yes. How'd you know?

We noticed them skulking around and overheard them talking about it.

What do we do?!

Relax. Phil, Claire, and Chris went to tell the adults.

Here they come now! We're saved!

Or doomed.

PLOP!

What happened?

Did the strangers attack you?!

Ooohhh. Cough.

No, we got caught in the rain. And then fell into the river.

We thought we couldn't get any wetter, but we were wrong.

Don't worry about the strangers. If they come here looking for trouble, we'll be waiting for them.

You don't look so good, Phil.

I'm fine.

Your nose is raining.

Studies of Neanderthal teeth tell scientists that Neanderthals ate their veggies — but also that they used medicines!

Plaque on teeth shows that some Neanderthals may have used plants that make aspirin and molds that make penicillin to treat illness.

Studies also indicate that Neanderthals weren't good at flossing!

So what's our plan?

What if we collapse the cave entrance on them?

Good idea, except then we'd be trapped in this cave forever.

We could wait until they're in the cave, THEN collapse the entrance and trap them?

Then they'd have all our stuff AND we'd have no home.

I've got an idea. Why don't we set a series of elaborate traps that bother and confuse them until they leave?

Yeah, we'll create a clever ruse to lure them in, just to surprise and scare them.

Guys, that's it!

See? Both of you have one good idea!

I wasn't serious.

Me neither.

They seem awfully pleased, considering our impending doom.

No, that's fake power. True power is hitting stuff hard, lifting heavy objects, throwing things really far...

Stabbing stuff. Breaking things...

Being strong isn't the only way to be powerful, Richard.

Oh? What else is powerful?

Working together, having a plan, using your imagination, and inventing things?

Pretty much all of those.

Yeah.

That's still only, like, one, two, three... four things. Name ONE more!

What about the element of surprise? Is that powerful?

Oh, definitely.

Thanks for letting us crash at your cave, kids.

We're NOT letting you.

If we make you let us in, you're still letting us in, right?

Fine. You can come in, but you should stay over here by the entrance.

That's the spirit, Reginald.

It's Richard.

But what if the wind blows the rain in a little? Shouldn't we move farther inside?

Ooh, there's a nice, warm fire back there.

That's better!

What do you think you're doing here?

scratch scratch

They're spreading their stink all over the cave.

161

163

166

167

THE END...
AND A NEW
BEGINNING!

HOW LONG HAVE WE BEEN HERE?

It's hard to imagine how long ago Neanderthals lived, or how long ago humans first appeared, or how long ago our ancestors first walked upright. It was a long, long time ago!

The universe is about 13.8 billion years old!

The Earth is about 4.5 billion years old.

Life on Earth first arose about 3.8 billion years ago.

Until just 600 million years ago, life was mostly one-celled organisms.

Dinosaurs first appeared about 230 million years ago.

Humans have been around just a tiny amount of time compared to some other life on Earth!

Dinosaurs ruled the Earth from 230 million years ago until about 65 million years ago.

Mammals have been around since about 210 million years ago.

The earliest ancestors of humans began to evolve about 7 million years ago.

Neanderthals and early humans appeared around 200,000 years ago.

Neanderthals went extinct about 40,000 years ago.

FAMOUS CAVES

These are some of the best-known caves where evidence of Neanderthal life has been found — and no doubt there are more caves waiting to be discovered!

LE MOUSTIER CAVE
Dordogne, France
Contained Neanderthal bones and flint tools, which have been named moustierien after the site

VINDIJA CAVE
Donja Voća, Croatia

Some of the best-preserved Neanderthal fossils in the world have been found at this site.

SHANIDAR CAVE
Kurdistan, Iraq
Held remains and artifacts of many Neanderthals, and evidence that they buried their dead

GORHAM'S CAVE
Gibraltar
One of the last known living spaces of Neanderthals!

REAL PALEONTOLOGISTS

Pam and Eric are book characters, but the paleontologists who have researched Neanderthals are actual people! These are just a few whose work helped me in writing the Lucy & Andy Neanderthal series!

RALPH AND ROSE SOLECKI investigated Neanderthal burials and helped change the concept of Neanderthals as primitive brutes.

SVANTE PÄÄBO decoded the Neanderthal genome and helped improve the science of paleogenetics.

KATERINA HARVATI'S research has included theories on modern human origins and the use of 3-D modeling in paleoanthropology.

CLIVE FINLAYSON has extensively studied the last-known sites of Neanderthals and their interactions with humans.

FRANÇOIS BORDES refined the study of stone toolmaking.

PAT SHIPMAN wrote about how early humans may have been helped by domesticating wolves.

MARY C. STINER investigated how Neanderthals interacted with animals and plants.

You might think you need to be a scientist to see real fossils, but even if you're not a paleontologist (yet) you can visit museums to start your training as an expert on Neanderthals and evolution!

MUSEUM OF HUMAN EVOLUTION
Burgos, Spain

Has an extensive collection of fossils and re-creations of hominin ancestors to tell the story of our human past

NATURAL HISTORY MUSEUM OF LOS ANGELES COUNTY
California, USA

Permanent exhibits include the story of evolution in the Age of Mammals and the massive Dinosaur Hall

MUSEUM OF NEANDERTHAL MAN
La Chapelle aux Saints, France

Exhibits related to the first discovery of a Neanderthal burial plus workshops and programs on Neanderthals and prehistory

FACT OR FICTION?

Lots of things in Lucy and Andy's story really happened thousands of years ago, but maybe not quite everything. What did scientists find out, and what was made up?

DID NEANDERTHAL CAVES HAVE ROOMS?
From studying artifacts found in different areas of caves, scientists have learned that Neanderthals had separate spaces for sleeping, eating, and making tools. They didn't have TV rooms, though!

DID NEANDERTHALS COLLECT FOSSILS?
Dinosaur fossils haven't been found alongside Neanderthal fossils, so it's highly unlikely. But paleontologists know that Neanderthals collected interesting rocks occasionally.

DID NEANDERTHALS EAT A PALEO DIET?
While the popular "paleo diet" of today includes eating a lot of meat, Neanderthals definitely ate their vegetables. They couldn't import organic kale from far away, though! Many vegetables and plants we eat today, like tomatoes, peppers, and broccoli, didn't grow in Europe and Asia when Neanderthals lived.

DID NEANDERTHALS PLANT CROPS?

Neanderthals ate plants, but didn't grow them. Humans first cultivated specific plants around 10,000 years ago. So Neanderthal kids never had the chore of weeding their vegetable garden!

DID DIFFERENT KINDS OF EARLY PEOPLE LIVE TOGETHER?

There's evidence that at least three groups— humans, Neanderthals, and Denisovans— lived together. There may have been more, but we're still learning the extent of their interaction

DID NEANDERTHALS ALWAYS LIVE IN CAVES?

It may seem that Neanderthals always lived in caves, but that's because most of the evidence we've found is in caves, where artifacts are better preserved. Artifacts from some open-air camps may mean Neanderthals slept under the stars more than we thought!

COULD NEANDERTHAL KIDS ACTUALLY OUTRUN A CHARGING WOOLLY RHINO?

No!

A FEW LAST WORDS*
FROM THE AUTHOR OF THIS SERIES

Me →

*Last words for <u>this</u> book — and until the <u>next</u> series!

There's a saying that those who forget the past are doomed to repeat it.

ROBOT HAS 373 TERABYTES OF MEMORY AND IS PROGRAMMED TO NOT FORGET.

If we can learn more about why Neanderthals went extinct, it can help humans today survive.

Fortunately, we have what Neanderthals didn't have: science and technology!

AND ROBOTS!

We can learn how we're affecting the climate, and how to stop hurting the environment we depend on.

Look, Andy. They did some... redecorating.

We painted all kinds of stories on the walls!

Nice! What's that one?

That's the time you fell in the river. And here's when you thought the mammoth poo was mud. And this is when you got scared by —

Giggle!

Are all these stories about me when I was a kid?!

Yeah! Mr. Richard and Mr. Tommy and Aunt Lucy told me ALL kinds of funny stories!

You know, maybe tomorrow I can tell you some stories about your aunt Lucy....

LOOK FOR THE STORY OF LUCY & ANDY'S GREAT-GRAND KIDS SOMETIME IN THE FUTURE!

Jeffrey Brown is the author of numerous bestselling Star Wars books, including *Darth Vader and Son*, and the Jedi Academy and Lucy & Andy Neanderthal series for middle graders. Fortunately, his cat is not scimitar-toothed.

jeffreybrowncomics.com
P.O. Box 120 Deerfield IL 60015-0120 USA

LUCY & ANDY NEANDERTHAL ROCKS!

From the author of the *New York Times* bestselling Jedi Academy series

LUCY & ANDY NEANDERTHAL

Jeffrey Brown

ACTUALLY, Neanderthals probably didn't have pet cats, because there were no house cats 40,000 years ago. The cats back then tended to be a lot bigger. Their pounces were much less friendly!

Cave lion

European jaguar

Nice kitties!

Ngandong tiger

The saber-toothed cat Smilodon didn't live in the same places as Neanderthals, but the smaller Homotherium — Scimitar cat — did. It wasn't as tiny as a house cat in reality, though.

Mreow?

Chill out with another Lucy & Andy adventure!